THE SECOND WIFE

THE SECOND WIFE

BRENDA CHAPMAN

RAVEN BOOKS
an imprint of
ORCA BOOK PUBLISHERS

Library and Archives Canada Cataloguing in Publication

Chapman, Brenda, 1955-
The second wife / Brenda Chapman.
(Rapid reads)

Issued also in electronic formats.
ISBN 978-1-55469-832-5

I. Title. II. Series: Rapid reads
PS8605.H36S42 2011   C813´.6   C2010-908119-6

First published in the United States, 2011
Library of Congress Control Number: 2010942254

Summary: A cop with a boring desk job tries to solve a case that might
save her ex-husband from a lifetime jail sentence. (RL 3.3)

Orca Book Publishers is dedicated to preserving the environment and has
printed this book on paper certified by the Forest Stewardship Council.

Orca Book Publishers gratefully acknowledges the support for
its publishing programs provided by the following agencies:
the Government of Canada through the Canada Book Fund and the
Canada Council for the Arts, and the Province of British Columbia
through the BC Arts Council and the Book Publishing Tax Credit.

Design by Teresa Bubela
Cover photography by Getty Images

ORCA BOOK PUBLISHERS
PO Box 5626, Stn. B
Victoria, BC Canada
V8R 6S4

ORCA BOOK PUBLISHERS
PO Box 468
Custer, WA USA
98240-0468

www.orcabook.com
Printed and bound in Canada.

14 13 12 11 • 4 3 2 1

For Ted, Lisa and Julia—with love as always

CHAPTER ONE

I don't know why I promised to meet the woman my ex-husband had left me for a year earlier. Maybe because she begged me. Maybe because I was curious. It might have been as simple as her choosing to meet at the Cantonese House restaurant a few blocks from the station where I worked. Lying Brian had ditched our twenty-two-year marriage for a woman from a temp agency he'd hired to sort out his sloppy filing system. It was time I met her and stopped imagining every possible way that she was a better wife than me.

My name is Gwen Lake. I am a forty-five-year-old divorced mother of none. I work for the Duluth police force doing bookkeeping and secretarial work when asked. I trained to be a police officer but never made it past this desk job. It turns out I have a talent for filing and numbers. I can read a document and remember details weeks later. Police Chief O'Malley says I keep the office running. He can't look me in the eye when he says it. I know he thinks women should be teachers or secretaries, not wearing uniforms and carrying guns. I am counting the days until he retires.

I got to the restaurant twenty minutes early. I picked a booth that gave me a good view of the front door. I wanted to see Marjory before she saw me. I'd only caught a glimpse of her once from a distance. It was the day she drove off with my husband into the sunset and out of our bungalow for the last time. But I was sure I'd recognize her.

She'd be young and big-breasted with *harlot* stamped all over her.

I pretended to read the menu while watching the doorway. It would have been good if I smoked so that I'd have something to do with my hands. Every time someone came in the door, my heart jumped. I was beginning to wish I'd stayed at work. In the end, I wouldn't have given a second glance at the five-foot-three redhead who walked my way after scanning the room. I would never have imagined that this was the woman who haunted my dreams and fueled my revenge fantasies. She just seemed so small and...ordinary.

"Oh, Gwen, it's good of you to see me. Brian described you to a tee." She slid into the seat across from me and shrugged out of her black trench coat. "We sure could use today's rain. It's been one hot dry month of May, hasn't it?"

Her troubled eyes were green, the lids painted blue. I placed her close to forty, and she was bony—like a chicken that needed fattening up. Her hair was copper-colored and held back from her face with a black velvet band that made her look young and vulnerable. I was beginning to see how Brian would have fallen for her. He was a sucker for helpless women. They stroked his ego and made him feel needed.

"And how did he describe me?" I asked. I should have known better.

"You know, mature. Medium height, blond and no interest in fashion..." Her voice trailed away and she looked around the restaurant as if making sure we were alone.

I sighed. Mature meant middle-aged. No interest in fashion meant frumpy. She'd cut me off at the knees without batting an eye. "So, what did you want to meet me about?" I asked, wanting to get the meeting over with. "You sounded upset on the phone." I raised a hand to the waitress to bring a couple of coffees.

Marjory swung her sad eyes my way. "I didn't know who else to turn to. You've been married to Brian and you're a police officer. I thought you'd know what I should do."

"Whatever are you talking about?"

"Was Brian at any time overly aggressive with you during your marriage?" Her eyes found mine and held.

"Brian! Brian aggressive? You have to be joking."

Marjory flinched but kept her eyes steady on mine. "I worried you'd react like this, but you have to believe me. Brian's changed since we got married. He's become so possessive, he frightens me. I need your help."

I blinked back the laughter tears once I saw she was serious. "Brian is the least violent man I know. I'm sure you're wrong about this." Not to mention crazy.

"He's changed," she repeated in a voice so small I had to lean forward to hear. "He's just not the man I thought I married."

"I could say much the same," I said, but the irony was wasted on her.

"I don't know who else to turn to," she whispered. "I think he wants to get rid of me."

"I'm probably not the best person to ask about that," I said. *Seeing as how I dream of getting rid of you myself.*

Maybe, in hindsight, I shouldn't have blown Marjory off as fast as I did that May afternoon. I could have listened to her fears and found out why she believed Brian was so angry. I should have gotten some details. But how was I to know that a week later Marjory's twenty-year-old son would report her missing and Brian would become the main suspect in her disappearance?

CHAPTER TWO

I was adding up the cost of new furniture for the chief's office when Cal Rodgers poked his head into my office, which was a tiny corner cubicle with a view of the parking lot. My office was at the opposite end of the hall from the police officers who worked patrol. The three detectives and the chief had closed offices down another hallway not far from me. I had a fan pointed at my face, trying to stay cool. The air conditioner had been broken all week and the building was like a pizza oven. It was the hottest July on record.

"Got a minute, Gwen?" he asked.

"Always got time for you, Cal," I said, mopping my face with a paper towel. I put down my pencil and watched him cross the floor toward me.

Cal was close to six feet tall and growing a bit of a belly. He hadn't shaved that morning and his beard was coming in gray. He perched his right butt cheek on the corner of my desk and asked me how I was doing. Cal had the red eyes of a drinker, but he was one of the sharper detectives on the force. I knew he wasn't really there to ask me about my health. I decided to wait him out. The sun cut through the blinds on my office window and laid a striped pattern across his grizzled face. He looked like a convict in a holding cell. Sweat beaded his forehead.

As predicted, Cal quickly got tired of the small talk. After a minute of silence, he looked me in the eyes and asked what he'd wanted to know all along. "So what's the scoop on Marjory White?" He waited, chewing on a toothpick. He squinted at me through the sun's glare.

"I don't know why everybody thinks something bad happened to her," I grumbled. "She probably just got tired of being married and left town."

"You could be right. But we may as well do the background. What do you know about her?" Cal was still friendly, but his voice had gotten a harder edge.

I sighed. "Not much. Marjory worked for a temp agency when she met my husband. Her duties included typing, filing and removing her clothes." I tried to sound amusing, but my words came out more bitter than I'd planned.

Cal mumbled something. It sounded like he had a hairball stuck in his throat. His dark blue eyes were regretful. He coughed and said, "Would you believe your ex, Brian, capable of harming her?"

"Not in this lifetime. Brian owns a shoe store for good reason. He'd rather crawl around on his hands and knees at someone's feet than face them head-on."

"Although, I guess we could safely say you didn't know him all that well since you were surprised when he up and left you," Cal said mildly. I noticed that his eyes had darkened from regretful to observant.

I slapped the side of my thigh. "Ha. Ha. Got me there," I said. "But fooling around on your first wife isn't the same as killing your second."

"Maybe, it's the start of the slide." Cal shifted and a stack of papers fell over. He tried to straighten them, but a second pile landed on the floor.

"Forget it," I said. "Touch one more thing and I'll have to handcuff you to the wall."

Cal smiled an apology before his mouth turned down at the corners. "You see,

Gwen, a woman's body matching the size of Marjory White was just found in the woods off Interstate 35. Too bad it's been such a hot summer. There's not much left of her. We're making an ID through dental records as I speak."

My heart felt like a can of pop that had been shaken and then opened. "It won't be her," I said. "There's no way that's Marjory."

"We'll have our answer soon enough." Cal grunted and pushed himself to his feet. "I'm sorry about all this, Gwenny. I know you and Brian were happy once."

"Yeah. Once upon a time, but I've moved on."

"That's good. Because it's not looking like there's much of that happily-ever-after shit for any woman stupid enough to marry him."

CHAPTER THREE

Two days later, Marjory White's body was ID'd, and the day after that Brian was charged with first-degree murder. Cal arrested him at home and put him in the city jail. His bail hearing was set for the following week.

As usual, the bad news traveled through the station like a head cold. When it finally reached me, I was sitting at my desk eating a ham and cheese sandwich. The shock hit me hard. I had to bend over and put my head between my legs, or I would have passed out.

Jan Hill from HR brought me a cup of tea and two stale cookies from a bag she kept in her desk drawer. She patted me on the back and said she was there if I wanted to talk. The detectives and patrol officers tip-toed around me all afternoon as if I was about to crack. Cal Rodgers wisely stayed in his office.

I spent the next two days going through the motions. Each morning I got up and put on the same clothes as the day before. Then I went to work and sat at my desk, staring into space. In the evenings I sat in front of the television and changed channels with the remote. I couldn't believe that a man I lived with for twenty-two years was a killer. I couldn't accept knowing that Marjory had come to me for help and I'd turned her away. The guilt weighed heavily.

By Thursday morning I'd had enough of grieving for the man I'd never really known and the woman who stole him from me. I stood in front of the bathroom mirror and shook my head. There were dark circles under my eyes. My face was pale and my hair was a mess. It was time for a shower and a day off. I had to pull myself together. "He's not worth it," I said to my reflection.

I stood in the shower and let hot water rain down on me for twenty minutes. Then I dressed in clean sweat pants and a yellow T-shirt. I walked into the kitchen and plugged in the coffee pot. Two cups and the fog began to lift.

I got the newspaper from the mailbox and settled at the kitchen table. I skimmed the pages, not letting my eyes rest too long on any disturbing articles about politicians or pretty actresses in rehab. I flipped to the personals section and kept skimming. My eyes doubled back. I'd almost missed the notice of Marjory's funeral above the real-estate ads. She was to be buried that afternoon in Forest Hill Cemetery. First, there was to be a private service in a downtown chapel.

I raised my head and looked out the kitchen window at the line of lilac trees at the end of our property. Brian and I had planted them the second year we lived in this house. He'd told me they'd keep growing long after we'd moved into an old-age home together. I'd believed everything he'd told me back then. It had taken me a long time to accept that he could throw away our life together.

My eyes dropped back to the newspaper. I reread the funeral notice several times. Brian might have turned into a lying little turd over the course of our marriage, but was he really a killer? Could somebody change that much in a year? The service was at two o'clock on the other side of town.

There was time to make it if I hurried. I jumped up from the table to go in search of my little black dress. I needed to get the lowdown on his late second wife. Her funeral service would be a good place to start.

CHAPTER FOUR

A handful of people were sitting in the front pews of the chapel. I slid into one a few rows back. The oversized blond boy sitting directly in front of me had to be Marjory's twenty-year-old son. I glanced over to my right in time to catch Cal Rodgers staring my way. I slowly rotated my head forward. It was common practice for the police to check out the funeral. But the sight of him bothered me somehow. It had to do with the pity I saw in his eyes before they hardened over and got impossible to read.

Hymns played softly over the sound system while we waited. Cold air was being pumped into the chapel. I shivered in my sleeveless dress. A woman in a light green pantsuit sat down at the end of my pew. She smiled at me briefly before facing forward. I tried not to let my eyes linger on the gold ring sticking out of her nose.

The chaplain's sermon was long and rambling. He talked about crossing over to a better place and embracing the light. All very generic. Marjory's name was inserted into the right places. Her son kept his head bowed the entire time. I could have sworn he was sleeping. That might have been because I caught myself nodding off once or twice. The chaplain became more animated delivering the closing benediction, and then the organist launched into one final hymn.

I had to shake my leg awake before I hurried up the aisle to catch up with my pew mate.

"Do you have a minute?" I asked.

She kept walking as if she hadn't heard me.

"I'm a police officer and have a few questions." Chief O'Malley would have had a fit if he'd heard me use that line.

The woman turned. She tilted her head to the door. "Outside," she said. She led me down the steps to a shaded piece of sidewalk. Then she lit a cigarette that she'd pulled out of her bag. After a deep hit of nicotine, she was ready to talk.

"Not sure if Marjory would have enjoyed that." Her pale eyes met mine, a trail of cigarette smoke connecting us. She had bleached hair and bright red lips. I put her just over thirty. "What I knew of her, she would have wanted something more elaborate."

"How'd you know Marjory?"

"We worked together. We both started at a temp agency a few years ago, but then she got married. She took several months off. Not long ago she came back. She only took the odd bit of work when it suited her. In fact, she was working a job just before she went missing."

"Sorry, what's your name?"

"Tina. Tina Sweet."

"Nice to meet you, Tina. Would you happen to know where Marjory was working last?"

"A dentists' office, but I don't remember which one. I was on holidays in Mexico with my new boyfriend Roy. He won tickets in a radio contest. We got drunk on tequila and stayed an extra three weeks. Just got back a few days ago."

"That must have been fun."

Tina sucked on her cigarette. "Marjory thought she was so brilliant marrying into money. She acted like she was better than the rest of us. Just goes to show."

"Brian...that is, from what I hear, her husband was doing all right but he wasn't exactly rich."

"When you have nothing, comfortable is a big step up."

"I guess you'll miss Marjory," I said, hoping she would say something personal. I tried not to stare at her nose ring. It was one of the biggest I'd ever seen.

"Nah, not really. I just came today because the boss couldn't. She said one of us had to show." Tina took another long drag. Then she flicked the butt onto the pavement where the tip lay glowing orange. "Well, if that's all, officer, I'm off. There's a cold beer waiting at home with my name on it."

CHAPTER FIVE

I followed Tina Sweet as far as the parking lot. I stepped around a flower bed to wait under the shade of an elm tree. I hoped to talk to Marjory's kid. My dress was sticking to me like flypaper in the heat. My sunglasses kept sliding down my nose.

Cal hurried past me a few minutes later. He was looking at the parked cars, one by one. I was sure he was trying to see if I was in one of them. I stayed very still and watched him get into his filthy blue Ford.

He took a final look around before driving away. He did *not* look pleased.

A few minutes later Marjory's son sped past me like he was late for a...I was thinking funeral, but that was just bad taste. I caught up with him as he was unlocking a black suv with tinted windows.

"Sorry for your loss," I said, catching my breath. "Lovely service though. Your mom is probably up there somewhere smiling down on you."

"Yeah, thanks." His eyes were pale blue and his blond hair reached just below his collar. He was a big boy—over six feet with a neck as thick as my two thighs tied together. Some women might have called him rugged. He kept sliding his eyes across me and around the parking lot. "How'd you know my mom?"

"We met over coffee a few times." I let my voice drop on the "few times" since

I'd only met her once. "She spoke fondly of you."

"Yeah, great. What was your name again?"

"Wendy," I lied. It was more of a fib than a lie. Gwen and Wendy were from the same name family. "Nice to meet you…"

"Jason."

"That's right, Jason. The last time I saw your mother, she told me how proud she was of you. She told me you were one terrific son." I winced. Maybe I was laying it on too thick.

Jason shifted from one foot to the other. His forehead was an accordion of puzzled lines. He lifted an arm to wipe his forehead and showed off a dark circle of sweat under his armpit. "She really said that?"

"Yeah." Time to change the subject. "Where will you live now, Jason?" I had to be careful not to ask for information a friend of his mother's should know. He looked suspicious enough, even if he didn't appear to be the sharpest tack in the box.

Jason pulled the suv door open and made to step inside without answering. Then he seemed to remember his manners. He turned and looked at me. "With my dad in Wisconsin. I'm going once everything with my mom is settled. I'm kind of in a hurry so I can't stay and talk."

"Well, good luck to you." I stepped back.

Jason climbed into the front seat and slammed the door. His tires sprayed up a shower of stones as he rocketed out of the parking space. In his beeline to the street, he narrowly missed hitting a flock of seagulls rifling through garbage.

CHAPTER SIX

It was time to pay a visit to my ex-husband behind bars. On a list of things I wanted to do, this came dead last. But I had to find out more about his marriage to Marjory. If he killed her, I needed to know. If he was aware of someone else who might have, that would be even better.

I drove home first and dug my police uniform out of the back of the closet. I hadn't worn it in several years. My desk job in admin didn't require a uniform. Luckily, it still fit, although it was snug in a few places best not mentioned. Then I made my way to the jail on Haines Road. I drove slowly. I wanted to arrive at four o'clock when shifts were changing. A little confusion would help me to pass through security.

Luckily, the kid on the sign-in desk was a summer student and easily impressed by my badge. Unluckily, I had to sign in. This meant Cal would find out I'd been to see Brian. If he wasn't happy to see me at the funeral, this would raise his blood pressure for sure. I waved off the kid's offer to get someone to take me to Brian's cell.

"Just point me in the right direction," I said.

Brian was lying down on his bunk when I stepped in front of his eight-by-eight living space. He was an average-looking man except for his doe brown eyes. I used to call them his Al Pacino eyes. They were the kind that made you want to keep on looking.

His face flashed surprise, then a smile when he saw me. He got up and came to stand a few feet from me, the bars between us.

"I don't know how you got around the no-visitor rule, but I'm glad you came," he said. "Sorry I can't invite you to sit down."

"Never thought I'd see you in an orange jumpsuit," I said. "I couldn't even get you to wear a pink shirt." I looked down the hallway. I dropped my voice. "I might not have much time. Sooner or later, they will figure out I'm not supposed to be here."

"What, no cake with a crowbar baked inside?" Brian grinned, but his puppy-dog eyes were worried. "You look good in uniform, Gwen."

"Yeah. But I smell of mothballs. So, anything you want to share about Marjory?"

The grin disappeared. "I had nothing to do with it."

"I don't think just saying so will get you off. Who do you think did it, if not you?"

"Believe me, I've been asking myself that. Marjory and I weren't getting along so great. After we got married, she said she'd made a huge mistake. She even moved me into the spare bedroom. I wish I'd…well, I wish I could take back the last few years."

I wasn't going to let him sidetrack me with regrets.

"Were you ever violent with her? Did you ever threaten her or hit her?" I watched him closely. He avoided eye contact and that set off alarm bells in my brain. I knew him too well. He was about to dance around his answer.

"I got angry, sure. She kept bugging me about stuff until I'd lose my temper. I never touched her though."

"What about her son, Jason?"

"That lump of useless space? He kept showing up and leaving. He and Marjory had a huge fight a few months after we were married. They seemed happier with each other when he came to stay in April.

He moved from the couch to her bedroom when she disappeared. I didn't feel right throwing him out until we found her."

"Who else was she fighting with?"

Brian thought for a moment. "She'd started a job somewhere and was working late a lot." He hesitated. "I think she was having an affair."

"*No!*" The sarcasm came from deep inside. "Not our Marjory."

He dropped his head.

"I deserve that," he said. "I've been a prime idiot."

"You won't get any argument from me," I said. "Has this new love interest got a name?"

Brian shook his head. "No, but she let slip that he's married with four kids."

I turned. A guard the size of the Hulk was coming down the hall toward me. I looked back at Brian. "Anything else you can tell me? Now would be the time."

"I think Marjory had a past. She wasn't who she seemed." He reached a hand through the bars. "I miss you, Gwen."

A beefy hand tapped me on the shoulder.

"Your supper will be along shortly," I said to Brian. "Next time you have a complaint with the food, suck it up." I spun around and nodded at the guard. "All yours," I said. "They don't make killers as tough as they used to."

I shook my head and stomped down the hall like I had somewhere to be. I didn't look back to see if the Hulk was following.

CHAPTER SEVEN

The next morning, I slipped into my cubicle unnoticed. I planned to finish some overdue accounting, then figure out what to do next about Marjory's murder. I filled in some numbers on a spreadsheet on my computer screen. As I typed, an idea hit me. I'd begin by phoning all the temp agencies in the city to find out where Marjory had worked. How many could there be?

I had the phone to my ear when Cal showed up in my cubicle just after nine.

He wore a green golf shirt and tan pants. He'd shaved and his hair was still wet from the shower.

"Going on a hot date?" I asked. "You're all prettied up. You smell like an ocean breeze."

Cal grunted. "Can I see you in my office, Gwen?"

"Now?"

"Now."

I followed him slowly. Cal was being even less charming than usual. It was a bad sign when he closed his door and pointed to a chair. He'd set the chair near the window where the sunlight shone on me like a heat lamp. I was sure it was no accident that he stayed in the cooler, shadowy end of the room. He absent-mindedly rolled a pencil on the desk as he talked.

"How come you were visiting Brian in jail yesterday?"

No beating around the bush with Cal. I shrugged. "Just making sure he couldn't escape. I think you should shackle him to the floor. Brian might want to do me next. You know, once you kill one wife…"

Cal didn't smile. He changed tactics. "Is there something about Marjory White you should be telling me?"

I thought back to our meeting in the Cantonese House restaurant. What could Cal possibly know? I shook my head.

Cal looked disappointed. His jawline tightened. "The thing is, Marjory White kept a diary. That's how we know she met with you on May twenty-first. I'd like to hear your take on the meeting."

Busted. I shrugged. "Nothing to tell. We had coffee. We talked. We laughed. I left."

Cal pulled a couple of papers from a stack at his elbow. He cleared his throat. He began reading, "'Met with Brian's ex, Gwen Lake, to discuss my growing fear that he is becoming angry and violent. Could tell she didn't believe me. Don't know where else to turn. I feel so alone.'" This time, Cal's eyes were definitely unhappy when he raised them to mine. I felt my insides squirm.

"Marjory had to be confused. Brian wouldn't hurt a fly, let alone someone he liked enough to marry."

"Her son Jason and a co-worker named Tina Sweet confirm her growing fear that Brian was going to hurt her. The last entry in her diary was a call from Brian to join him for lunch at a restaurant...near Interstate 35. It was the last time anyone saw her. She recorded the meeting in case something happened."

"Wow. That sure looks bad for Brian," I said, my mind not catching up to my mouth. Why hadn't he told me this when I saw him in jail? "So I guess you're not looking too hard for other suspects."

"Not when we have such overwhelming evidence."

"But, there's no motive."

Cal spoke slowly, as if I was a child who'd failed a test. "There's always a motive if one partner wants out of a bad marriage."

His words got me thinking. People mostly kill for love, money or revenge. "Who inherits his business and home?"

"If Brian gets convicted of killing Marjory, it all goes to the kid, Jason. He's the next of kin." Cal picked up a thick brown file folder and began flipping through the report. "There's also a life insurance policy with Jason named as the beneficiary. Marjory took out the policy before she married Brian. She told her lawyer she was going to change the name over to Brian. Looks like she never got around to it. Kid's lucky."

"How much is that worth?"

"Half a million. The boy won't be suffering money-wise anyhow."

"Well, that gives Jason a motive. Why aren't you looking at him?"

"The kid loved his mother. It's in almost every page of her diary. No way Jason killed her for half a mill."

"Don't forget about the store and condo."

"Jason told me that he thought his mother had changed her will. He believed everything would go to Brian. He was as surprised as anyone when he found out he was to inherit."

"How convenient."

"Listen, Gwen." Cal ticked off his fingers as he made the list. "Marjory was scared of Brian. Even you have to admit that. She and Brian were not getting along. Brian was the last one to see her alive. He set up a meeting at a restaurant about a mile from where we found her body. We also know that he was capable of lying. Look at how he treated you. Any more evidence and he'd come tied up with a bow and a sign saying *wife killer.*"

"I guess," I said. I wasn't convinced.

"I'm going to ask you to stay out of this, Gwen. Stop nosing around. Maybe book off some holiday time. Go on a Club Med cruise and put this whole sorry mess out of your mind."

"I'll think about it," I said. I watched him put Brian's file on his desk. A thought was forming in my brain that Cal would definitely not like. "I should just leave this to you to solve," I said. *Big strong you with all the brains.* I resisted batting my eyes.

Cal smiled for the first time since he'd appeared at my desk. "That's right, Gwenny. I need to work without stumbling across you everywhere I look. You have to let the expert handle this. I've got everything under control."

"I'm breathing easier already," I said.

CHAPTER EIGHT

I waited until Cal and the other detectives left for the night. I stayed at my desk an extra fifteen minutes to make sure Cal wasn't coming back for something he'd forgotten. He sometimes went for supper nearby and returned to work. Something told me that was probably what he was up to this evening. That would give me a half hour tops to do my snooping.

The cleaning lady was down the hall emptying garbage cans when I snuck into Cal's dark office. The overhead lights were on a motion sensor. They clicked on when I stepped inside. I crossed quickly to his desk. Marjory's file was not where he'd left it. Could he have taken it with him? I rifled through the remaining papers and folders but came up empty.

I circled the room. I flipped through files stacked on the window ledge and piled up against the wall. The clock was ticking. I raced toward the filing cabinet and tripped over a briefcase. It was on its side next to the desk. I knelt and popped open the catch. Relief flooded through me. Marjory's file was on top. I scooped up the folder and headed to the photocopier next to my cubicle.

I knew what I was doing could get me fired. Cal had always been friendly with me, but that would mean nothing. He wouldn't take kindly to anyone messing with the evidence. He had a reputation for being tough and relentless when working on a case. The other detectives always said that they were glad not to be one of his suspects. I could only imagine what he would do if he saw me copying the file.

As the copier ran off the pages, I studied the crime-scene photos. Cal hadn't been kidding when he'd said there wasn't much left of her. I would never have recognized this as the woman I'd met a few months before. The summer heat had done its work. A wild animal or two had done the rest.

The printer finished and I stuffed all the copies into my big handbag. I ran back to Cal's office and put the file back inside the briefcase. I tried to put the case back exactly as it had been. I heard the cleaner talking to someone down the hall. I hunched over and scooted out of the office and around the corner. I glanced back and saw Cal bent over the water fountain. This gave me time to keep going down the hall to the exit. I hoped that he wouldn't notice the overhead lights on in his office. Maybe he'd think it was the cleaner who'd been inside.

I drove home as if I was being chased. I ran a red light before I calmed down. I'd even tucked my handbag out of sight under a blanket in the trunk. My fear was that Cal would notice that somebody had gone through his papers. He'd have to figure out that I was the only one interested. He'd track me down and throw me in the cell next to Brian.

None of this happened.

I made it home without being stopped. I ran inside, locked the door and set the house alarm. Then I closed the curtains in the living room and spread the file out on the coffee table. I settled myself on the couch with a glass of red wine and a yellow highlighter.

I read through all of the evidence and statements. I stopped only long enough to heat up a frozen dinner in the micro-wave. I wolfed it down while looking at the shadows in the backyard through the kitchen window. I thought I saw a flash of white behind the raspberry bushes in the corner of the yard. I kept watching. A plastic bag blew from the bush and across the grass toward the house. I let out my breath. For a minute I'd pictured Cal lurking in the bushes, waiting to arrest me.

I carefully read through the file a second time. I learned that the body had been wearing Marjory's wedding band. Jason had recognized what was left of the clothes. That would have confirmed the positive ID from the dental records. The dental X-rays were also in the file. She'd been strangled. Jason had reported that his mother and father divorced when he was twelve years old.

He'd moved with his mother to an apartment on Oak Street three years ago. Before that, they'd lived in Ohio.

My eyes were getting blurry. I packed up the papers and hid them in the bookcase. Then I went to bed.

I had trouble falling asleep with all the information swirling around in my brain. I dozed, but it was a fitful sleep. When the birds started singing, I gave up trying. I staggered into the kitchen and made the coffee extra strong.

I poured a cup and sat at the kitchen table, thinking. The information replayed in my head like a series of pictures. By the second cup of black coffee, I'd come up with a plan. The file had given me the first place to start digging. It was the Hampton Temp Agency—the place Marjory had worked when she met Brian. According to Cal's notes, the owner was a woman named Sally Peters.

I stood up to fill my cup again. I'd make some eggs and toast to go with it. Then I'd get dressed and spend my Saturday playing detective.

CHAPTER NINE

S ally Peters was unlocking the door when I drove into the parking lot. She held a coffee in one hand with a newspaper tucked under her arm. I stepped out of my car and walked across the parking lot toward her.

"Do you have a few minutes?" I asked. "I'm with the police and have a couple more questions about Marjory White."

She glanced at the badge I flashed at waist level. Then she pushed the door open. "Why not? You're lucky to have caught me. I just came in today to catch up on paperwork." She was a tall woman with bristly orange hair and a hooked nose. Her red workout outfit had a designer logo. Gold jewelry dripped from her ears, neck and arms. The woman was making money, no doubt about that. I wondered how much her employees were being paid. Probably not enough to buy the bling hanging around her neck.

We stepped inside. She and a trail of strong perfume led me into her office. I sat down across from her with a desk between us.

"Sad news about Marjory," she said. She raised the coffee cup to her lips. "Horrid way to go, really." She didn't sound all that broken up.

"I understand she met her husband through your agency."

Sally leaned closer as if telling me a secret. "I hate to gossip about my staff. Still…you are the police. He wasn't the first client she dated. I never knew what men saw in her. Each to his own, I guess."

"Would you say she was looking for a man?"

"No. Well, maybe." Sally laughed. "Aren't we all?"

"She kept working after she was married?"

"Not at first. About three months ago she phoned and asked what I had." Sally pulled out a file and traced down the page. "Last two jobs included a doctors' office and a dental clinic." Sally looked up. "She told me that she wasn't working for the money. She said it was difficult at home. Her husband was jealous. Working was the only reason he'd let her out of the house."

"Are you sure she said that?"

"As sure as I'm sitting here. To be honest, I don't think he should have thought work would keep her from meeting somebody else. She knew her way around men."

"Was she good at her job?"

"She was my best worker. I thought sometimes that she was too smart to be hired as a secretary. She told me once that she'd stayed home to raise her son Jason. That's why she didn't go further in school."

"Did she ever talk about her ex-husband?"

"Just that they divorced when Jason was twelve. They didn't keep in touch."

"I met Tina Sweet at the funeral. She didn't seem too close to Marjory."

"Well, they used to be friends when Marjory started working here. They'd go shopping or to the bar after work. Then they got upset with each other over something. I have no idea what. They weren't really friends when Marjory died. There's not much else I can tell you. I did most of my talking with Marjory by phone or email. I don't get together after work with the help as a rule."

The help. That's rich. "I wonder if I could get a photocopy of Marjory's record."

"Is it important?"

"It might be. I won't know until I've finished all the interviews."

"Then you're welcome to it. I can't see her filing an objection anytime soon."

"No, I'd say her complaining days are all but over," I said.

CHAPTER TEN

When I returned to my car, I glanced through the papers that Sally had given me. They included the address Marjory had when she first moved to town. Before she got her claws into Brian. It was time to find someone who knew more about her past.

I started the car and headed toward the south end of the city. It was a fifteen-minute drive. I used the time to think about what angle to take with people in the building. Should I be a police officer or pretend to be a friend from Marjory's past? Which would get me more information?

The apartment building was four stories—brown brick, late seventies. The balconies were rusted iron. The front door and windows were original to the building. Marjory had lived on the second floor. I got in easily enough. The front-door lock was broken, and the door opened when I pulled the handle. I climbed the stairs to the second and looked around. Marjory's apartment had been the one at the end of the hall. The apartment next to it had a wreath of faded plastic flowers on the door. I took this as a good sign that the tenant had lived there a while.

The woman who answered my knock was white-haired and tiny like a bird. "Can I help you, dear?" she asked.

"I'm looking for a woman I think lives next to you. Her name is Marjory White. She doesn't appear to be home."

"Goodness. She hasn't lived there in over a year." The woman's smile disappeared.

"I hate to tell you, dear, but I just read in the paper that she died."

"No! I can't believe it." I was ashamed at lying to this trusting old woman. I had to remind myself why I was there.

She opened the door wider. "You've had a shock. Come in for a cup of tea. It'll make you feel better."

"You are very kind," I said. I stepped inside the apartment.

"My name is Rose Gatto," she said. "Make yourself at home while I pour the tea. I just made a pot before you knocked." She shuffled to a galley-sized kitchen. I followed her.

"Let me help you," I said. I took the tray and carried it to the coffee table. I set the tray onto a stack of magazines.

Rose took her seat in the rocker. I cleared a space to sit on the couch across from her. Boxes of dishes and kitchen gadgets, clothes still in packages, books and ornaments were stacked everywhere. A plastic Christmas tree stood on top of the TV. Pink and red valentine hearts hung from the ceiling. Rose waved a hand to take in the room.

"I keep buying things. It's that damn shopping channel. I have trouble sleeping, and those smiling salespeople keep me company. It's nice to have a real live person to talk to."

"Have you lived here long?" I asked. It seemed a silly question when I looked at all the junk.

"Dear me, yes. I moved here in 1984. It was just after I retired from teaching. I turned eighty-three last month. Don't think I'll move unless I have to. Still have my wits about me."

"Are you able to get around okay?" I asked.

"Well, I don't like to complain. I have a niece who brings me food once a week. A woman from the church comes for tea on Tuesday mornings."

"There's a seniors' center not far from here," I observed.

"No way to get there." She drank some tea. Then she set her teacup down in its saucer. "But you've come about Marjory. I read about her murder in the paper. A terrible end for that young lady."

"We weren't all that close. I only met her through my ex-husband. I'm wondering if you remember her. I understand she lived at the end of the hall for a year or so."

"Marjory and her fella moved in two years ago October. He came and went for the first few months. Then he stopped coming. It was a few months after that when she moved out."

"I think you mean her son Jason. I'm told he came and went all the time."

"No. I know who Jason is. This was a different man. Older and smarter. I think it was her husband."

I was puzzled. "But she was divorced." Maybe Rose wasn't as sharp as she looked.

Rose looked at me as if I was the slow one. "Divorced or not, you don't have to be married to sleep together. For certain they were having relations."

I nodded. I'd skip over that one. "So how was Marjory as a neighbor?"

"I had her for tea once or twice. She was a cagey one. Told me she came from New York, but I knew that was a lie. Her accent was local. She had a girlfriend that used to visit up until April. She was younger than Marjory but they could have been sisters."

"I think they worked together. Was her name Tina Sweet?"

Rose tilted her head. She stared at me again as if I had a screw loose. "No, this woman was named Alice. They knew each other from a long time ago."

"Did Marjory tell you anything about her past life?"

Rose chuckled. "No need. I've seen her kind before. She used people. Sorry to speak ill of the dead." Rose's teacup rattled as she lifted it from the table. Her eyes were shiny buttons behind her glasses. "She tried to get me to give her money. Don't look so surprised. I'm old and she thought she could put one over on me. She stopped coming around when she didn't get me to hand over my bank account information."

"That's terrible." This clinched it. Marjory had used Brian too. He'd been even stupider than I thought. No wonder he couldn't look me in the eye.

We finished our tea and Rose talked about the kids she had taught. She had a special fondness for the ones she called rascals. I thought that the kids must have been lucky to get her for a teacher.

"You've been a big help," I said as I stood to leave. I looked down at her. "I'd enjoy if you'd come with me to bingo next Saturday evening at the seniors' center. I read a notice in the paper this week.

They're looking for new players. I could pick you up and bring you home."

Rose's face lit up. "Why, I'd enjoy that. I used to like a night out."

I returned her smile. "I'll come by to get you around seven."

CHAPTER ELEVEN

I thought about what I'd learned as I waited for my frozen dinner to cook in the microwave. Marjory came to town without much money. She was a liar, and if Rose was to be believed, a thief. She had fights with her son and her co-worker Tina Sweet. Brian thought she had started having another affair.

I sighed. Everything I'd found out about Marjory gave Brian even more reason to kill her. I could either give up in defeat or keep turning over stones. If I gave up looking, Brian would go to jail for a long,

long time. It also would mean that I should have listened to Marjory when she begged for my help. I would have to spend the rest of my life knowing I might have saved her. Both ideas were difficult to accept.

I decided to dig deeper into the last months of her life. The documents that Marjory's boss gave me listed the recent employers—a doctors' office and a dental clinic. The next day was Sunday. The offices would be closed. I'd have to wait until Monday to pay them a visit.

I sat with the plastic tray of fried chicken, potatoes, green beans and applesauce in front of my computer screen. I clicked on Google. A search gave me Tina Sweet's address. She lived not far from me. I'd drop in on her tomorrow afternoon. That should give her time to recover from the hangover that she probably was working on getting right that moment.

I decided to take the night off. I called a girlfriend, then my brother in Boston. After that I went to bed and dreamed I was in an eight-by-eight cell. Brian stood on the outside of the bars, waving at me. He was holding a chocolate cake. I got up off the bed and walked toward him. I was relieved to see him. I knew he was there to save me. When I reached the bars, he pressed his face close to mine. He smiled and whispered into my ear. He thanked me for killing Marjory and giving him back his life. He said that she'd deserved to die.

*   *   *

Tina Sweet lived in a townhouse on Wildwood Drive. I parked on the street and walked to the front door. It was just past one o'clock. I hoped she was up.

I was surprised at how full of energy she looked when she opened the door. She was wearing a denim miniskirt and halter top. Her face was scrubbed and her bleached hair was tied back. She had taken out the gold nose ring. Her smile disappeared when she saw it was me. She looked over my shoulder as if expecting someone else.

I flashed my badge. "Sorry to bother you, Tina. We met at the funeral service. I just have a couple more questions about Marjory White."

"They have the guy who did it."

"I'm just tying up loose ends."

"Well, come in then. Let's get it over with."

We sat at the kitchen table. Tina lit a fresh cigarette from one burning in the ashtray. "Is your boyfriend here?" I asked.

"Who? That guy I went to Mexico with? Roy and I broke up the day of the funeral."

"I'm sorry."

"Don't be. He didn't look as good once I sobered up. So what are your questions?"

"I'm curious about something. You were friends with Marjory until something happened. Could you share what it was?"

Tina shrugged. "I guess it doesn't matter now she's dead. It was because I started dating her son, you know, a while ago."

"Jason?"

"Yeah. He's not a great talker, but he's lots of fun. Not hard on the eyes either."

I was speechless for a moment. Jason wasn't what I would call attractive. Alcohol must have lowered her standards. "Is that why she and Jason were fighting too?"

"Oh yeah. Marjory acted like I was a home wrecker. She wanted me nowhere near her son." Tina shrugged. "I ended it with Jason. Seemed the best way to keep Marjory from declaring all-out war on me."

"Interesting. Do you know if Marjory was having an affair when she died?"

"Not sure. But she sure did everything possible to take that dental-clinic job away from me. Sally gave it to me first. Then Marjory kept asking for it until Sally gave in. It was odd."

"Why?"

"Well, it meant Marjory had to drive clear across town to work. She already had a nice job near where she lived. Maybe she had her eye on one of their dentists and was waiting for an opening." Tina flicked cigarette ash onto the table. "Is that all? I've actually got a date. He should be here any moment."

"Yes. That should do it."

We walked toward the front door. "If you think of anything, here is my phone number." I handed her a card with my name and office number.

We stepped outside. Tina waved at someone across the street. He was just locking his car parked behind mine. I ducked my head, but it was too late. Jason had seen me. He looked puzzled, like he was trying to place me. I glanced at Tina, and she wouldn't meet my eyes. It hadn't taken her long to get back with Jason now that his mother was out of the picture. Curiouser and curiouser.

I hurried to my car and climbed inside. I locked the door and drove away without making eye contact. I prayed he wouldn't remember seeing me in the funeral home parking lot. Before I turned the corner, I saw Jason hugging Tina in my rearview mirror. Talk about an unlikely couple. They seemed as good a match as a cow and a chicken. Marjory had freaked out when they were dating. Both had been angry with her for breaking them up. The way I saw it, they had two good reasons to want her out of the way—money and hormones. These motives were enough to make them suspects in my book. But did they have what it took to kill her?

I hit my forehead with the palm of my hand. How stupid could I be? I should never have left Tina the card with my name on it.

Jason would see it and know that I wasn't an old friend of his mother's. He might even have heard my maiden name from Brian or his mother.

Once again, I drove home as fast as my car could manage. I kept checking to make sure I wasn't being followed. It seemed like a good idea to lie low for the rest of the day.

CHAPTER TWELVE

Monday morning I made it in to work for eight. I planned to catch up on some work and then visit the dental office. I'd brought the papers that Sally Peters had photocopied for me. It was time to figure out where the dentist office was located. I skimmed down the sheet until I found the clinic name. "Pine Tree Dental on West Superior Street," I read aloud. I lifted my head. Some bit of information was floating in my memory bank. "Aha! Marjory worked at the same place where Cal got the dental records to ID her."

I looked around to make sure nobody heard me talking to myself. I tossed the paper back on the desk. It was a little fact that might mean nothing. It was just one more useless bit of information that wasn't getting me any closer to saving Brian. I knew that I should just stick to my desk job and stop playing detective. But the puzzle had me in its grip.

Cal came by my desk as I was getting ready to leave for the clinic. It was close enough to noon that I could claim the time away as my lunch hour.

"How you doing, Gwen?" he asked. He stood in the doorway to my cubicle. He looked uncomfortable.

"Do you want a real answer or a cheery one?"

"Yeah. Not much happiness around here lately. Anyhow, I just wanted to be the one to tell you that Brian didn't make bail. It's a first-degree murder charge."

"You sure know how to pick up a girl's spirits."

"Sorry, Gwenny."

"Did Brian say he met her that day? You know, at the restaurant near Interstate 35?"

"They were seen together. He claims she called him. He also says she was alive when he left her. However, we found her blood in the trunk of his car. Nobody ever saw her alive again after they left the restaurant together."

"I don't think he did it, Cal. I was married to the man a long time. I would have known if he had the killer gene."

"Anyone can crack. I wish it didn't look so bad for him."

"Yeah." I grabbed my handbag from my desk and stood up.

"Can I buy you lunch, Gwen?"

"Maybe another time. I have a dental appointment."

"Okay. Don't let them drill too deep."

* * *

I slid my car into an empty space underneath a giant plastic molar suspended from a metal pole at the north end of the parking lot. It was a short hot walk past a takeout pizza place and a store offering two-for-one body piercings. The doors to Pine Tree Dental slid open in front of me. I headed for reception.

I had to wait for a man with slobber dribbling out the side of his mouth to finish paying by credit card. He sounded like he was chewing on waxed paper. He left and the girl motioned me forward. She had a microphone strapped around her head that she spoke into every now and again. It was as if she was talking to a secret lover who whispered into her ear. Her name tag said *Cindy*. A big-toothed smiley face was pinned to her chest.

"Yes. Can I help you?"

"I'm here about Marjory White."
I flashed my police badge.

Cindy's eyes got rounder. "Such a sad thing. We could hardly believe she died. It's been a tragic month. Just tragic."

"I'm here to collect her file."

Cindy's forehead wrinkled. "Why, we gave her X-rays to the police already." She leaned forward. Her voice lowered. "I believe they had to identify Marjory by her dental records. Her body was cooked by the heat." A delicate shiver ran through Cindy's shoulders.

"Yes, but I'm looking for Marjory's entire record. The file doesn't have her dental history."

"We still haven't found it if that's why they sent you back. Dr. Williams told that detective we'd call if it showed up. Sorry." She spoke into her headset. "No, he cancelled. You have a root canal at two." She turned back to me and flashed me her perfect white smile.

I leaned on the counter as if I was settling in for a chat. "So, how well did you know Marjory?" I asked.

"Marjory replaced Brit. Brit was hit by a car and broke both legs, so we had to use a temp agency. Lucky that a card for the Hampton Agency arrived in the mail that week. Anyhow, Marjory showed up and we were impressed. She volunteered to stay late and sort out the files. We miss her."

I pretended to hesitate. "Cindy, you seem like a person who can keep a secret. There have been rumors brought to our attention that Marjory might have been seeing one of your dentists. I wonder if you can confirm this information."

"Seeing how?"

"Seeing as in dating. Having a relationship." Boinking.

Cindy laughed. "No possible way. Three of our dentists are women and married. The other dentist is a man but definitely not interested in women." She puffed out her chest. "I can attest to that personally."

"No married dentist with four children works here?"

"Nope."

I was confused. I'd been sure Marjory was having an affair. Why else would she have demanded to work here? Too many random events had happened with Marjory at their center. My mind was making connections but they weren't adding up. I needed to find out more about her past. That meant tracing back through her life and anyone who knew her.

"Do you happen to know who her last dentist was before she transferred here?"

Cindy's face clouded over and then brightened. "I only remember because I overheard her cancel an appointment when she first arrived and thought what a small world. Dr. Bloom is my mother's dentist too. That's why his name stuck in my head.

He's not taking on new clients though. He plans to retire in the fall."

"Thanks so much for your help," I said. I tapped the counter twice with the palm of my hand. "Have a nice day."

I put my head down and trotted for the door.

CHAPTER THIRTEEN

I'd gotten behind on my work at the station. The chief wanted some forms filled in before I left for the day. That put my investigation on hold. I sat at my desk typing in information with a knot of frustration in my stomach. It was hard to concentrate on paperwork when I would rather be tracking down clues on Marjory's murder. My mind had been sprung out of a box, and I couldn't put it back in. The thrill of the chase and the excitement of solving a puzzle had given me energy.

I now had a reason to get up in the morning. I hadn't even known what I was missing. I wondered if I would ever be happy sitting at a desk again.

The nightshift had arrived by the time I stepped outside. It was still daylight, but the sun was on its way down. I wasn't paying much attention to anything as I walked toward my car. I was thinking about Brian and what a sitting duck he'd been. He was a middle-aged man working in a shoe store. Marjory had played on his memories of youth—offered him a chance to find the excitement long gone. It made me sad to think he hadn't tried to find it in our marriage.

I waved at two police officers heading out on patrol. I just needed to make a few more phone calls before I had all the information to prove how the murder had happened. I was starting to like being a detective. It was exciting when the facts began to make sense.

It wasn't until I reached the parking garage that I noticed somebody behind me. I'd caught movement out of the corner of my eye. My first thought was to run, but I didn't want to go deeper into the garage. I'd be trapped like a bug in a jar. I turned to face whoever was standing across the sidewalk from me in the shadows. I could make out a man's shape but not his face. He stepped forward and started running toward me. It was a shock to see Jason bearing down on me like a tank. His face was red and angry. He was bigger than I remembered.

"Can I help you, Jason?" I tried to sound in control. Even so, I could hear my voice tremble. I put my hands on my hips. I wouldn't let him know that he scared me. For the first time since I took the desk job, I wished I had my gun. It was locked up in a safe at home. There'd been no need for a gun or a uniform when I was doing paperwork. I looked around. We were alone and all but hidden from view.

Jason stopped a few feet away from me. "You told me you were a friend of my mother's. Then I find out you're a cop, asking about her murder. I also find out you were married to Brian. You lied to me." He shouted the last bit. His fists were clenched at his sides. "Your name isn't Wendy. It's Gwen Lake. You must have thought you were so smart lying to me."

"I should have been more honest. I'm sorry. I was just helping the detective."

"Brian killed my mother."

"I know. All the evidence points to him."

"Then why are you still asking questions?"

"I'm done as of today."

Jason's shoulders relaxed. "Good because I want Brian to pay for what he did."

"Oh, I'd say he's paying already."

Jason nodded. "You know when you asked me where my father lives and I said

Wisconsin? Well, I meant New York. I get confused."

"That's okay. Geography isn't my strong suit either." If a girl needed to roll over and play dead, I could give lessons.

"Okay, well, I just wanted you to know that you shouldn't be tricking people. Some of us don't like it. We might have to stop you."

"Consider me stopped. It was wrong of me to act like I was friends with your mom."

Jason started to back away. He looked confused. He'd probably been expecting more of a fight. "Okay," he said. "I guess I'll see you around then...or not." He cocked his hand at me like he was firing a gun. "Just so long as you leave me alone."

"You can count on it."

He turned and started walking away from me. I held a hand up to cover my wildly thumping heart. I watched him until he was gone from sight.

"Got you worried, Jason?" I whispered. "It seems that I'm making you sweat. Now what's that all about?"

I turned and started walking toward my car. Tomorrow I would track down the last few people I needed to talk to. I'd start with the doctors' office where Marjory last worked. I needed to find out if she was having an affair with one of them. I would follow every lead to the end. I knew I was getting close. But I was still a long way from bringing the killer to Cal on a platter.

CHAPTER FOURTEEN

Doctors Anders, Neil and Carlson had a booming practice, judging by the number of people in the waiting room. It was eight AM, and I thought I'd beat the morning rush. I was wrong.

I walked up to the woman behind the glass divider and waited until she got off the phone. She was late forties with curly black hair and coffee-colored skin. Her eyes said smart and no-nonsense.

"Which doctor are you here to see?" she asked.

"I'm not sure. I'm here to make an appointment."

"I'm sorry, but none of the doctors is taking on new patients at this time."

"But I was told that one was. I just forget his name."

"Well, we have two male doctors on staff. Dr. Anders and Dr. Carlson."

"Marjory said the doctor I should ask for had four kids."

"Marjory?"

"Marjory White. She told me to mention her name." I stole a look at her name tag. "She said that Pam would be able to help me out."

"Well, I'm Pam. I guess you haven't heard. Marjory White died a few months ago. I hope you weren't too close." There was no sadness in her voice.

"Oh my god! This is such a shock. I just knew her from the gym. I wondered why she'd stopped coming. She told me that she liked working here." It was scary how easily I'd taken to lying. It was like a hidden talent.

If a face could snort without snorting, Pam somehow managed it. "I'll *bet* she liked it here. I was as surprised as anyone when she took another job." Pam leaned closer. "Dr. Carlson is the one with four kids. She chased him like a dog in heat. She was always staying late, trying to cozy up to him. It made me sick."

"Did Dr. Carlson fall for her?"

"At first I'd say he was…flattered. Marjory was good at roping them in. I'll say that for her. He seemed to like the attention for a while. Then he found it disturbing. He told me after she left that he was going to let her go."

"Maybe he was just covering his tracks."

"No. The last few weeks that she was here, he was going home early to avoid her. He loves his wife."

"So he resisted Marjory's charms," I said.

"You could say that." Pam held up a finger as she picked up the phone. She called to one of the patients to take waiting room two. Then she said, "I can't say I was shocked she ended up murdered. There was something nasty about her. She came across so sweet and needy with the men. But Dr. Carlson saw through her. Most middle-aged men probably wouldn't have. I know it's awful to speak ill of the dead. It's just that women like Marjory get me going. They waltz in and break up families and couldn't care less."

"You're preaching to the converted," I said. I couldn't help myself. I added, "Marjory gave women a bad name."

Pam smiled for the first time. "If you really would like an appointment with Dr. Carlson, I can put your name on the waiting list."

"Thanks. I'll take you up on that. Dr. Carlson sounds like the kind of man I'd like having for a doctor." By the sounds of it, I should have picked him for my husband too.

* * *

I was late to work again, but nobody noticed. My in basket was loaded with files. I moaned at the sight of them. I worked through lunch. There was no chance to make my phone calls until late in the afternoon.

Rose Gatto picked up on the first ring. "Any progress on Marjory's case, dear?" she asked.

"Some. I have a few more questions for you."

"Fire away. I got nothing but time."

"You said that a man used to visit when she first moved in. What did he look like?"

"He was in his fifties. Rough-looking. Bald with a five o'clock shadow. There was a tattoo of a rose on his left arm and a scar across his left cheek under his eye."

There was nothing wrong with Rose's eyesight. Sadly, she wasn't describing anyone I knew. I checked back through my notes. "You also said she had a girlfriend named Alice."

"She and Alice spent a lot of time together. I'd say that Alice was in her late thirties. She was short and mousy. I never saw what the two of them had in common."

"Do you know her last name?"

"I was never formally introduced. However, my window looks out over the visitor parking lot. She had a vanity license plate that said *Coates*. That would be my guess."

"Alice Coates. I seem to remember seeing that name somewhere." I couldn't place where, but I'd read her name recently. I was too tired to think.

"I never saw her again after Marjory moved out."

"Well, thanks again, Rose. Are you still up for bingo on Saturday night?"

"Yes, dear. I'll be waiting downstairs. I ordered a new dress a few nights ago. Some fancy fabric that they wear on the moon. The lady on the Shopping Channel said it would make any body type look twenty pounds lighter."

"I should have gotten you to order me one. I have a few craters that could use some slimming moon fabric."

Rose giggled. "Wouldn't we be a sight. The two of us showing up to bingo in the same dresses. Like we were trying to be twins or something." She was still chuckling when I hung up the phone.

I sat without moving. My mind was sifting through information, making connections. I let out a whoop. The last piece of the puzzle had just slotted into place.

"Rose, thank you, thank you," I yelled. I grabbed my handbag. If I hurried, I might be able to get to wrap this up before closing time.

I felt like a bloodhound on the scent. I hardly recognized my bright eyes and the determined set of my jaw in the elevator mirror. An old man with a cane stopped and raised a hand to give me a thumbs-up as I passed by him at the entrance to the station.

CHAPTER FIFTEEN

A few hours later I knocked on Cal's apartment door. He wasn't thrilled to see me. "How did you know where I live?" was how he put it.

"I spend my days reviewing forms. I've seen your address so many times, I know it like my own." I stepped inside. Kids' toys were scattered down the hallway. Cal kicked aside a fire engine and dump truck as he led me into the living room.

"I looked after my niece's kids the last few evenings so she could have a break," he offered as way of explanation. "Her mom, who is also my sister, lives in another state. I was recruited by my sister to keep an eye on Valerie and the grandkids."

"I never figured you for the babysitter type." I grinned.

"Not only is Valerie my niece, but she also made me her boys' godfather. She wanted to be doubly sure I'd be on call when needed."

I pulled a half-eaten red sucker from the cushion before sitting down.

"Don't tell me. Val and Cal. Your niece was named after you, and your sister was a fan of Dr. Seuss."

"What can I say? She likes names that rhyme." Cal clicked off the television with the remote. He sat down at the opposite end of the couch. "So what couldn't wait until the office?"

How to begin? Always start with some sugar.

"You've put a solid case together to prove Brian killed Marjory. I have to agree the evidence is all there."

"Good to hear."

"But..."

"I've got a feeling I'm not going to like what comes after the *but*."

"*But* I know Brian. I needed to convince myself because he was the kind of guy who caught flies in the house and let them go outside. It was hard to believe he'd kill a person in cold blood."

Cal's eyebrows rose together in an untidy arc. He sighed deeply.

"I knew you were up to something. I hoped whatever you found would help you to accept what Brian did."

"Actually, I've found evidence that proves Brian is innocent."

Cal clicked on the TV and muted the sound. His eyes fixed on the baseball game.

"Lay it on me then…tell me what *brand-new* evidence you've come up with all on your own."

"Okay, I will." I ignored the sarcasm. I turned on the couch so that I was facing him. "Marjory White wasn't the woman she appeared. She lied about everything."

"So?"

"Too many things about her weren't adding up. Why did she want us to believe that she moved here from New York, but her son Jason goofed and said Wisconsin? Why did she demand the job at Pine Tree Dental when she had a doctor in her sights? And maybe strangest of all, why did she marry Brian? He owns a shoe store, but he's not exactly a babe magnet."

"She fell for Brian and married him. Then they fell out of love. He got angry and she found out he had a violent streak."

"Brian is not violent. She set him up and I can prove it."

"*Please*, fill me in."

"The first real thing that tipped me off was when I found out there were no married men at the dental clinic. Add to that, it was way across town from where she lived. Why did she insist on working there? She even switched her dentist to one at the new clinic. She wiped out the file that gave her dental history. I noticed it was missing in the records from Pine Tree."

"How did you know where we got her records?"

"Oh, I might have read it somewhere." I waved off the detail with a flick of my hand. It seemed best to hide the fact I'd copied his case file. "Marjory was laying the trap."

"I'm still not following." Cal was running a toy car up and down his leg. His eyes were fixed on the silent television screen.

"It got me wondering why she'd gone to all that trouble. Then it hit me. Marjory needed to work and be a patient there to switch the records—the dead woman's for hers."

The toy car flew across Cal's leg and clunked against the wall on the other side of the room. Cal sat up straighter. I had his attention. "The problem with your logic is that we don't have another dead woman."

"But I think you do. Marjory had a girl-friend from her hometown named Alice Coates. Alice was the same size as Marjory. In fact, I was told by a reliable source that they could have been sisters. Alice didn't have any family in Duluth. Marjory prob-ably looked Alice up when she moved here." I took a deep breath. "Marjory and Jason killed Alice and cleaned out her bank account. They dumped her remains beside Interstate 35 and put her dental records in Marjory's file. I checked. Alice was a patient at Pine Tree Dental. Someone reported that she moved to Florida. None of her family in Wisconsin has heard from her."

"How do you know that?"

"I remembered her name. We opened a file on her a few months ago. A cousin in Wisconsin phoned the station to say they were worried. Nobody had heard from her. One of our guys looked into it and said there was no crime. I entered the data into the system. The officer reported that she'd quit her job and cleaned out her apartment and bank account. Everyone thought she'd moved south. There's no law against not telling your family."

"But she hadn't?"

"No, she was already dead. Marjory and Jason kept her body somewhere to give it a chance to, uh, cook. Then they dumped her not too far from the restaurant where Marjory asked Brian to meet her. Marjory lied in her diary. She wanted you to believe that Brian had invited her to the restaurant. After that lunch, Marjory left town and pretended to be dead. They even put some of her blood in the trunk of Brian's car to make it look like he'd murdered her." I was on a roll. "When Marjory worked at the clinic, she stayed late to put Alice's dental X-rays into her file. That way, you'd match the teeth from the body with Marjory's dental records. Remember, it was Jason who identified the wedding ring and what was left of the clothes."

"Well, if what you say is true, the teeth should also match with Alice's X-rays in her real file."

"I shook my head. Alice Coates's dental file is missing. I already checked."

Cal was sitting forward, his elbows on his knees. I could see him replaying the evidence in his mind. "If this is true—and I'm saying if—where is Marjory now?"

"I believe she and her real husband are hiding out somewhere. They're waiting for Jason to collect on the life insurance policy. He's also supposed to sell off Brian's business and condo when he's found guilty. Then Jason plans to join them."

Cal closed his eyes. His face had paled. "There's no way to prove any of this."

I reached into my bag. "They made a few mistakes. I visited Marjory's old dentist, Dr. Bloom. When Marjory left, she took her file with her. She also erased it on the computer in Bloom's office. She didn't know that it had been backed up on a disc. She worked weekdays and wasn't aware that one of the girls made a disc every Saturday. Here's the disc with Marjory's real X-rays. They won't match the ones in your file. I'm sure of it."

"You said *mistakes*, as in more than one?"

"They didn't count on a lonely old woman living next door to their first apartment.

Rose Gatto remembers Alice Coates and Marjory's real husband. He used to visit Marjory before they found a mark. Brian to be exact. The other thing that Marjory hadn't counted on was Jason's affair with her co-worker Tina Sweet. Marjory got angry with Jason and made him break it off. He could have blown the whole deal."

"I'm guessing you have all this documented?"

I reached in my bag and handed him the file I'd been gathering.

He looked down, then back at me. "I can see I have some work to do."

"Like find out where Marjory and her husband are living."

"That's top of my list. If all this checks out, Brian owes you big-time."

"All in the line of duty," I said.

I reached the front door and turned. Cal was already talking into his cell phone and slipping one arm into the sleeve of his jacket.

His eyes met mine. I could tell he believed me. He had the look of a bloodhound tracking a new scent.

I smiled and let myself out.

CHAPTER SIXTEEN

By late Friday morning, Jason was sitting in the Duluth jail. It didn't take him long to spill his guts. He'd helped his mother kill Alice Coates. He and his mom had moved to Duluth to get a fresh start after some money went missing at her previous job. Marjory came up with the plan to clean up on her insurance only after a chance meeting with Alice at the mall. She remembered how people used to confuse the two of them in high school. It took her a while to work out the details. She used the time to reel in Brian. He was to be her backup plan.

Jason gave Cal his father's address in a little town in Wisconsin. His father was living a few towns over from where Marjory and Alice grew up. Cal called the Wisconsin state police. They picked up Jason's dad before lunch. They also arrested a woman who turned out to be the very much alive and kicking Marjory.

I sat at my desk. The excitement of the chase was over. I felt as deflated as a balloon after a nail had been poked into it. The past week had made me realize how empty my life had become since Brian left. I had a boring desk job and nobody waiting at home. My life sucked.

Jan Hill from HR stopped by for a chat. "Have you heard the big news?" she asked. "Cal broke the Marjory White case wide-open. He figured out that she faked her own death and pinned it on your ex, Brian. Her son Jason killed a woman who looked like Marjory. Marjory and her son even managed to switch dental records. They would have gotten away with it if Cal hadn't kept digging. He's like…a hero."

My mouth fell open. I could feel anger shoot up from my stomach. I couldn't breathe. For a few moments I thought that I was having a heart attack. I made myself inhale deeply and pushed the anger back down. There was no use fighting. Of course Cal claimed the victory for himself. He couldn't let himself be outsmarted by a desk officer. "Cal's a cracker all right," I said.

I was a loser and it was time I accepted it.

The rest of the day dragged. I couldn't concentrate on my work. All I wanted to do was go home and sit in front of the TV with the remote and a bottle of wine.

Midafternoon, the inbox on my computer dinged. An email message had arrived from the chief. I clicked it open and skimmed the words. He wanted everyone to meet in the boardroom at three o'clock.

I sighed and deleted the message. O'Malley was always sending emails to the wrong people. He should leave computer tasks to his assistant.

At ten after three, I received a phone call. It was the chief's assistant. She told me that I was late for the meeting and they were waiting for me. Everyone on staff was expected. Even little old me.

I hurried to the room with a pen and notepad. I tried to slip in without being noticed. The only empty seat was between Cal and Chief O'Malley. Neither of them looked at me when I sat down.

O'Malley stood up to speak. He was a short bald man but tough as they come. He'd been chief for the past ten years. "I am letting you know today that I've promoted Cal Rodgers to assistant chief," he said. "Cal has done outstanding work on many files. The Marjory White case is the latest example. I'm also letting you know that I'll be taking a long vacation beginning next week."

Everyone laughed. They clapped for Cal. I managed a couple of claps but my heart wasn't in it. I felt more like using my hands to slap him.

Cal stood up and raised his arms for silence. "Thank you, Chief O'Malley. As you know, I headed up the White case. We had a surprising but satisfying end to the case. I'm happy to take the credit...but I can't because I didn't solve it. Gwen Lake put the clues together and handed me the killers." He reached down and pulled me to my feet. "Gwen is the true hero on this file." His eyes were twinkling.

I staggered against him as he pulled me into a hug. Cheers and clapping broke out. A few officers whistled. I stepped back and held a hand to my mouth.

"I've asked the chief," Cal continued, "and he's agreed to promote our Gwen to junior detective. We can use her talent to help solve future cases."

O'Malley stood and shook my hand. "Welcome to the detective division, Gwen," he said. "Cal says you did some very good work."

* * *

Brian was sitting on my front steps when I made it home. I was later than usual because Jan Hill and I had gone for a drink to celebrate my promotion. I parked the car and walked toward him. He was tired but smiled and stood to hug me.

"Cal tells me I owe you."

"You're welcome," I said. "Do you want to come in for a minute?"

We got a couple of beers and sat in lawn chairs on the back deck. It wasn't as hot as it had been all July. There was a nice breeze cooling things down.

After a while, Brian said, "I'd like to come home. I miss you and our life.

What do you say, Gwen? Can you give me another chance?"

I took my time answering. I thought about the twenty-two years we'd lived together. I remembered the pain when he left me. I'd been lonely when he was gone. But I'd made it through Christmas and my birthday and holidays without him. I fixed my eyes on the lilac bushes. They'd grown a good foot over the summer.

"I say that it's too soon. I'm not ready to be married again or to have you back in my life. You need to sort out your life too. There was a reason you fell for someone like Marjory White. We owe each other some time."

Brian took my hand. "Sometimes, we take for granted what we've got," he said. "The grass isn't always greener."

We drank our beer and sat outside until the sun set and the bugs came out. Then Brian got up to leave. I could hear his footsteps long after he disappeared into the darkness. I sat a while longer listening to the night sounds.

I stood and stretched my hands to the sky.

"You're going to be a detective," I said out loud. It was the first time I actually believed it. Laughter started deep in my belly and bubbled out of my mouth. I laughed so hard that tears rolled down my cheeks. I threw back my head and looked at the stars. I yelled at the sky, "Gwen Lake, the forty-five-year-old couch potato is making a career change! Take that world!"

Then I grabbed the empty beer bottles and stood up. I twirled twice around the deck before I danced my way into the house.

BRENDA CHAPMAN is the author of the murder mystery *In Winter's Grip* (2010), along with the successful Jennifer Bannon mystery series for young adults. She is a former special education teacher and currently works as a senior communications advisor in the federal government in Ottawa, Ontario.

 **RAPID READS**

The following is an excerpt from
another exciting Rapid Reads novel,
And Everything Nice by Kim Moritsugu.

978-1-55469-838-7 $9.95 pb

When honesty isn't always the best policy.

Stephanie manages a clothing store and lives with her
mother in the townhouse where she grew up. Her life
isn't in a rut exactly, but it's not headed where she'd
like it to be. Things begin to look up when she joins
a community rock choir and meets Anna Rai, a local
TV personality. When Anna's personal journal goes
missing and ends up in the hands of a blackmailer,
the two women lay a trap to snare the crook.

One day, a few years ago, I found a wallet in the parking lot of the mall where I worked. It was sitting on the ground, open, right under the driver's door of a BMW. Like it fell from the driver's lap when he got out of the car and he didn't notice.

The wallet bulged with cash. Four hundred dollars' worth. And credit cards, a bank card, a driver's license. Everything.

I picked it up and looked around. Was anyone running back to the car in a panic? Nope. The parking lot was empty of pedestrians. And the spot where I stood was out of sight of the mall's outdoor video cameras. No one would see if I slipped the wallet into my bag and kept walking. Or if I removed the cash and dropped the wallet back on the ground.

I stood there for a minute and considered those options. And others. I could leave the wallet where I found it, money and all. Or I could write a note, stick it under the windshield wiper, and turn the wallet into mall security. But I didn't trust some of the guards who worked there.

In the end, I left a note with my name and my cell number. I took the wallet into work. An hour later, I handed it—contents intact—to a relieved man who matched the picture on the driver's license. As soon as he got it, he pulled out a fifty-dollar bill and gave it to me.

"Thanks for your honesty," he said.

I took the fifty. Who wouldn't?

CHAPTER ONE

My mom, Joanne, heard about the community rock choir from her teacher friend, Wendy. I heard about it from Joanne. So no wonder I wasn't interested. Not that I didn't get along with my mom. I did. I mean, I was twenty-four and working full-time as manager of the Gap store in Fairview Mall. But I still lived with her in the townhouse where I grew up.

Joanne liked my company. I liked not paying rent while I was saving to buy a car. For a fifty-five-year-old mom, she was pretty chill. And I was pretty easygoing.

I always have been. Except for when I was nineteen and dropped out of university after one semester. And refused to ever go back.

We were over that, and things were all good between us. But I didn't want to join a choir that met on Tuesday nights in a church and sang rock music. I didn't even like rock music. I was more into pop and urban, top-40-type tunes.

"There *are* pop tunes on the play-list," Joanne said. This was one night in September after the choir's first practice. She came home, warmed up the Thai food I'd ordered in, sat down to eat it and raved about the fun she'd had. "'I Gotta Feeling' by the Black Eyed Peas, for instance. You like that song, don't you?"

"I liked it when it was current."

"And there's a Pointer Sisters song. Talk about music from my era."

"Who the hell are the Pointer Sisters?"

"And there's something by Journey on the list, and 'Honesty' by Billy Joel. I love that song."

"Billy Joel? Are you kidding me? Next you'll say the choir's singing Elton John."

"How did you know?"

"Look, I'm glad you found something to do that you like. A bunch of people your age singing classic rock just doesn't sound like my scene. At all. No offense."

She sagged in her chair. "Oh, Stephanie."

I hated when she said my name like that. Like I'd disappointed her. "What?"

"You were such a good singer when you were little, such a born performer. I think you'd like the choir."

She also thought that by working in retail, I was throwing away some bright future I could have had. The kind of future university grads have.

"I'm not a good singer," I said. "I never was. You just thought I was good because you're my mom."

"How about if you come to choir practice next week and try it, one time? The choir members aren't all my age. Some are in their twenties and thirties. And Wendy and I are in the soprano section. You wouldn't have to hang out with us, or even talk to us. You'd be an alto or a tenor with your raspy voice."

I picked up my phone from the coffee table and pretended it had vibrated. "I missed a call from Nathan. I should call him back. I'm working twelve to nine tomorrow, so I'm staying at his place tonight."

"Say you'll at least think about the choir. I'll pay the fee if you join."

She had that right.

"I'll think about it. I promise."

"Good. Could you pass me my wallet? It's in my purse, on the floor. I want to give you money for the Thai food."

I fished out the wallet and waited while she picked through the receipts, ticket stubs and dollar bills she had stuffed into it.

She said, "That's weird. I thought I had more cash than this. Did you take some out of here already?"

"How could I have done that? I just handed you the wallet two seconds ago."

"I meant before I went to choir practice."

Was she losing her mind? "I wasn't here before your practice, remember? I got home from work after you left. And ordered the Thai food. As you instructed."

She shook her head. "So you did. I'm sorry, I wasn't thinking. Here." She handed me a ten and a twenty. "I thought I had more cash on me. I must have spent it somewhere."

"I love how your first thought when money is missing is that I took it."

"I said I was sorry." She smiled up at me. "I used to take money from my mother's wallet all the time when I was a teenager— a five here, a few singles there. She never noticed."

"Well, I'm not a teenager. And I guess I'm more trustworthy than you were."

So far I was anyway.

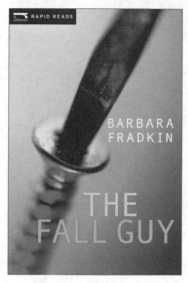

978-1-55469-835-6 $9.95 pb

If necessity is the mother of invention, fear might be its father.

Handyman Cedric O'Toole likes his simple life. He lives by himself on a hardscrabble farm, collecting sheds full of junk and dreaming of his next invention. But all that changes when he discovers the lawsuit he's been slapped with for faulty workmanship might turn into a manslaughter charge.

RAPID READS

978-1-55469-282-8 $9.95 pb

"My name is Rick Montoya. But you can call me the spider. Other people do."

When Rick Montoya returns to the city to try to clear his name, he discovers someone is living in his apartment. Before he can find out who it is, the apartment house goes up in flames. Was the firebombing meant for him? Who exactly was killed in the fire? And why? What was his landlady doing at home in the middle of the afternoon? The questions mount up, along with the suspects.

RAPID READS

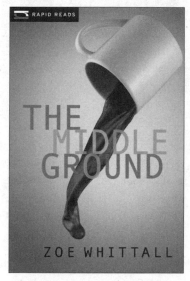

978-1-55469-288-0 $9.95 pb

When everything goes wrong at once, Missy Turner begins to make some unusual choices.

Missy Turner thinks of herself as the most ordinary woman in the world. She has a lot to be thankful for—a great kid, a loving husband, a job she enjoys and the security of living in the small town where she was born. Then one day everything gets turned upside down—she loses her job, catches her husband making out with the neighbor and is briefly taken hostage by a young man who robs the local café. With her world rapidly falling apart, Missy finds herself questioning the certainties she's lived with her whole life.

Titles in the Series

 **RAPID READS**

WLHS Library Media Center
58 South Elm Street
Windsor Locks, CT 06096
860-292-5736

DATE DUE
